THE BIG BED

Farrar Straus Giroux Books for Young Readers
An imprint of Macmillan Publishing Group, LLC
120 Broadway, New York , NY 10271

Text copyright © 2018 by Bunmi Laditan
Illustrations copyright © 2018 by Tom Knight
All rights reserved
Color separations by Embassy Graphics
Printed in China by Toppan Leefung Printing Ltd.,
Dongguan City, Guangdong Province
Designed by Kristie Radwilowicz
First edition, 2018
10 9 8 7 6 5

mackids.com

Library of Congress Cataloging-in-Publication Data

Names: Laditan, Bunmi, author. | Knight, Tom, illustrator.
Title: The big bed / Bunmi Laditan ; pictures by Tom Knight.
Description: First edition. | New York : Farrar Straus Giroux, 2018. |
  Summary: A young girl tries to persuade her father that he is the one who
  should sleep in a special, little bed while she shares the big bed with
  Mommy.
Identifiers: LCCN 2017006023 | ISBN 9780374301231 (hardcover)
Subjects: | CYAC: Bedtime—Fiction. | Parent and child—Fiction. |
  Beds—Fiction. | African Americans—Fiction.
Classification: LCC PZ7.1.L22 Big 2018 | DDC [E]—dc23
LC record available at https://lccn.loc.gov/2017006023

Our books may be purchased in bulk for promotional, educational, or business use. Please
contact your local bookseller or the Macmillan Corporate and Premium Sales Department
at (800) 221-7945 ext. 5442 or by e-mail at MacmillanSpecialMarkets@macmillan.com.

FOR M, T, AND F,
WITH LOVE FROM MOMMY
—B.L.

FOR RÓISÍN AND TEDDY
—T.K.

THE BIG BED

WITHDRAWN

BUNMI LADITAN

Pictures by **TOM KNIGHT**

FARRAR STRAUS GIROUX

NEW YORK

I am a reasonable person.
I don't want to see anybody
get their feelings hurt.

Daddy, please sit down.

I have no problem with you during the day.
You're a wonderful wrestler. You're also very
gifted at the art of the horsie ride.

What I'm trying to say is that you are
a valued member of this team. A VIP.

But every night, we struggle with the same question:

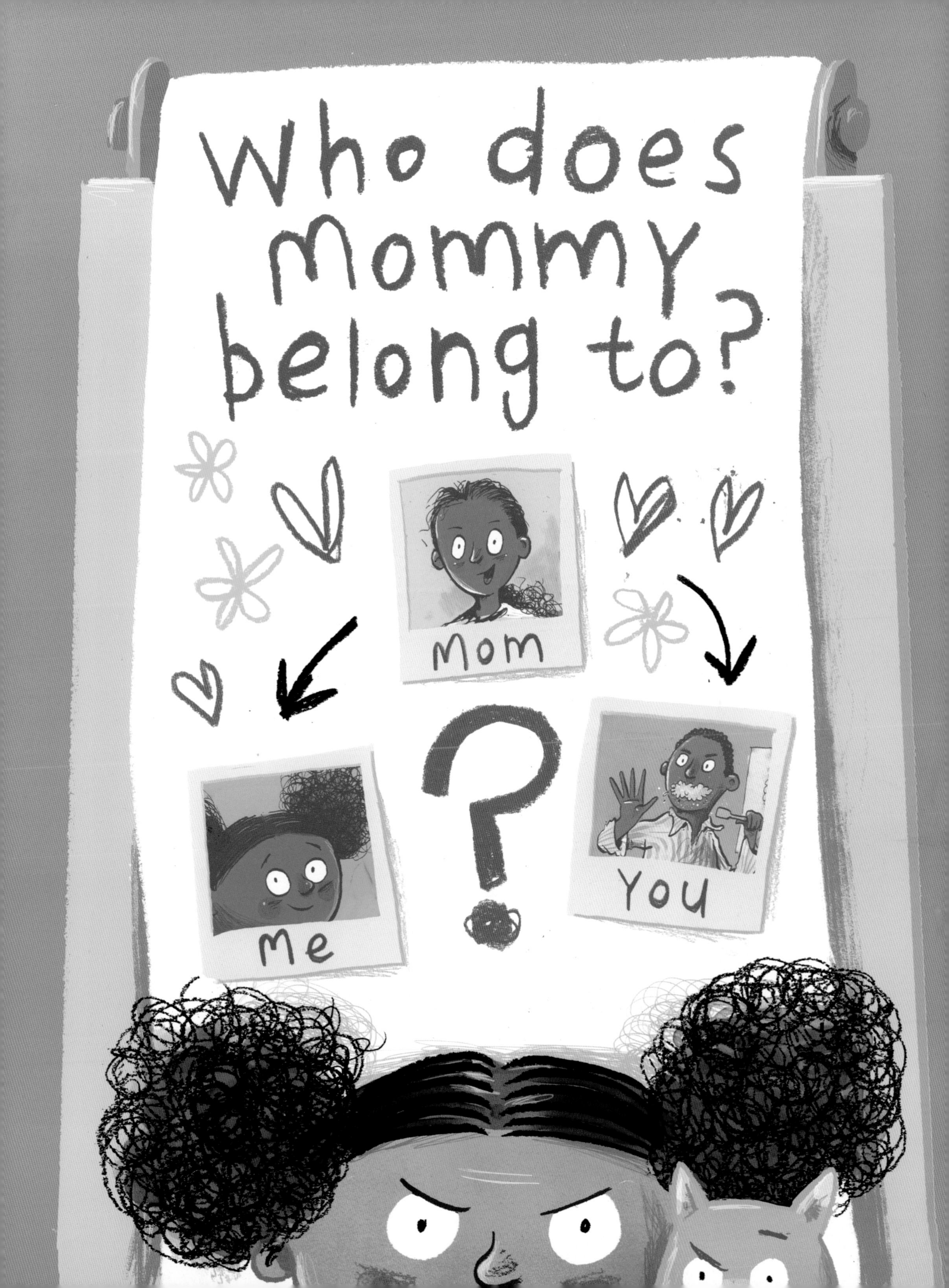
Who does Mommy belong to?
Mom
Me
You

When day turns to night, it's normal for people to seek comfort. No one can deny that Mommy is full of cozies and smells like fresh bread. **Who wouldn't want to cuddle with her?**

Seeing as how there are two of us but only one
of her, we face a hard decision.

Quick question: Am I mistaken, or don't you already have a mommy? Perhaps Grandma is available to sing you to sleep three or four nights a week? I'm almost positive she'd be willing to tap your back for a few minutes.

Science has proven that one of the many symptoms of bedtime is **darkness**.

day time   bed time

Grandma

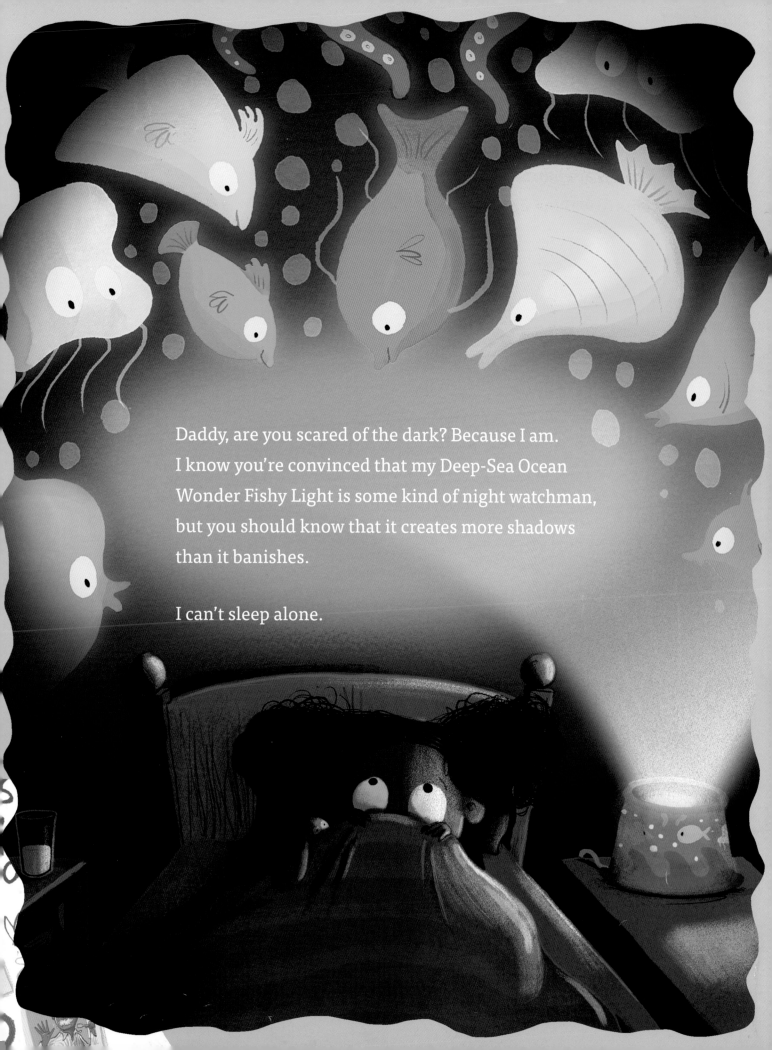

Daddy, are you scared of the dark? Because I am.
I know you're convinced that my Deep-Sea Ocean
Wonder Fishy Light is some kind of night watchman,
but you should know that it creates more shadows
than it banishes.

I can't sleep alone.

Delicate question: Is it the pee-pee? I looked it up online and you'll be thrilled to know that my tinkles are harmless. There are actually many benefits to waking up damp from liquid waste:

You'll repel bears during the day.

Ammonia smells are nature's alarm clock.

No need to shower, you're already wet.

Space is definitely an issue. I appreciate how you try to squish your body into the far lower-right corner of the bed, but that's no way to live. Besides, you need a restful night's slumber to prepare for a day of text messaging and telling me "No."

Daddy, I see you.
I hear you.

You'll be thrilled to know that I've come up with a
solution that you are sure to find not only satisfactory,
but also quite generous, if I do say so myself.

Every night can feel like a camping trip with a metal-and-canvas cot! With this almost twin-size portable mountain bed, you'll feel like an honorary park ranger and look like one, too!

Look, this one's even on sale!

Okay, okay, Daddy, hold on. I can already feel your
resistance. You don't have to start out the night sleeping on your
special nature box. We'll all cozy up together in the big bed and
once you're nice and asleep, Mommy and I will *gennnnnnnntly*
roll you onto your big-boy bassinet. It will be right next to ours if
you need anything. Anything at all.

Except being next to us.
You can't have that.

In the morning, feel free to come join us again.
Quietly, though, okay? We're resting.

I presented this idea to Mommy earlier
and she laughed and laughed, which I
took as two thumbs up.

I hope you're as excited as I am. Tell you what: Tomorrow, we're going to pick out some special new sheets for your awesome sleeping rectangle.

Mommy and I just want you to be happy.